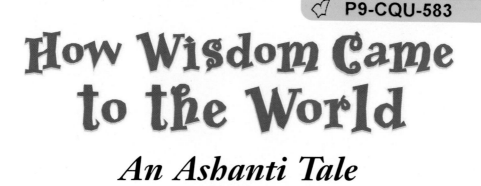

How Wisdom Came to the World

An Ashanti Tale

retold by Benjamin Khan
illustrated by Marla Baggetta

 HOUGHTON MIFFLIN   BOSTON

A long, long time ago, no one in the world had any wisdom. People and animals wandered around, trying to understand what life was all about. Sometimes they would learn things, but they would forget them quickly. There were no wise creatures. Anansi the spider was not wise.

One day, a visitor came to Anansi's spider web. It was Nyame, the sky god. The spider was surprised because he did not often have visitors.

"Hello, my friend," said Nyame. "I have some gifts for you. I have some sweet yams and a golden thread for your web." Anansi reached for the gifts, but the sky god continued speaking. "In return, I need a favor, if you please."

The sky god carried a pot under his arm. Nyame pointed to the pot and said, "This pot contains all the wisdom in the world. Please take it and share the wisdom with everyone. I cannot do it myself, because a thunderstorm is coming, and I need to get ready. So please do this favor for me."

Anansi was lazy and did not really want to help. But he did agree to help Nyame. He was pleased that Nyame had asked for a favor. He was also very curious about the pot and what was inside of it.

As soon as Nyame left, Anansi pulled off the pot lid and looked inside. "Oh, my!" he said.

The pot contained many wonderful secrets. Anansi looked at the secrets carefully. As he saw them, he became wiser and wiser.

Anansi learned where fat flies sleep and how to catch them. He learned how to make cloth from bright threads. He learned how to make colorful pottery. He learned where to find gold in the ground. He even learned how to gather plantains and how to make yams grow larger and sweeter.

At first, Anansi planned to share this wisdom with all the other creatures, as Nyame had asked. But when Anansi saw all the secrets, he became greedy and wanted to keep the secrets for himself.

Why should I give away any of this wisdom? he thought. *I will keep it all for myself!*

Then Anansi started to worry. What if someone saw his pot, lifted the lid, and looked inside? Anansi decided to hide the pot.

Should he hide the pot in the river? No, the pot might float away in the river.

Should he hide the pot on the plains? No, a grass fire might burn the plains, and the pot would be destroyed.

Anansi tried to think of a safe place to hide the pot.

Just then, Anansi noticed a tall tree. *Aha!* he thought. *I will hide the pot up in this tree, where no one will see it.*

Anansi picked up the heavy pot and started to climb the tree. He did not get very far because it was too difficult to hold the pot and climb at the same time.

"This is no good," he said. "I need all my eight hands just to hold this slippery pot."

Anansi thought more about his problem. Finally he decided to pour all of the wisdom out of the pot and into a gourd. He loosely tied the gourd to his waist with a rope. "Now I will be able to climb the tree!" he said, smiling.

Once again, he began to climb. But the gourd hit him in the stomach. Then it hit his chin. Later, it hit him in his eye.

12

Anansi looked up the tree to the good hiding place. It was still far away. His stomach, chin, and eye hurt. By now, Anansi was feeling tired, cross, and unhappy.

Just then, a young girl passed by the tree. She looked up and waved. Anansi frowned at her.

"Why are you angry?" the girl asked.

Anansi didn't know if he should answer for a moment. Then he said, "I want to climb to the top of this tree, but this gourd keeps hitting me. Look at my eye and my chin!"

"I have an idea," the girl said. "Tie the gourd tightly onto your back. That way, it will not hit you, and you can climb up easily."

Anansi stared at the girl with his four eyes. Why hadn't *he* thought of that?

I have all the wisdom, Anansi thought, *but I couldn't solve my problem. This girl solved my problem easily.*

Anansi wondered why he was having so much trouble. Was it because he had not followed Nyame's directions about what to do with the pot?

Anansi decided this was too much work for him. He frowned and looked up at the sky. "This is what I think of your wisdom!" he shouted to the sky god. Anansi angrily threw the gourd down from the tree.

The gourd landed on the ground and shattered into many little pieces. Bits of wisdom went everywhere. The wind picked up some pieces and dropped them all over the world. People found the bits of wisdom and took them home.

Today, you can find wisdom everywhere. Everyone in the world has some of it. Wise people, who have more wisdom than other people, have learned to share what they know. No one person has all of it.

That is how Nyame's wish came true. Now, everyone in the world shares all the wisdom in the world.